The Bourbon Street Musicians

The Bourbon Street Musicians

by Kathy Price

Illustrated by
Andrew Glass

Clarion Books
New York

To Judy, DeWayne, and especially you, Ali,
the three muses … I love you more than anything.
−K. P.

To Kevin, Vincent, Thomas, and Meghan,
my four noisy friends.
−A. G.

At the first cockcrow, just about the break o' day, an old jack mule stood creaking in a cornfield. He'd been gentle to ride and could drag a wheel, but the years had caught his gray hairs, and now he was obliged to earn his mash as a scarecrow.

Hour upon hour he troubled the crows, stomped his feet at horseflies, and ducked the sun, a blue velvet hat with a red silk rose dangling over his ear.

At first the nearsighted crows were so frightened, they brought back every kernel of corn they had stolen. But when they realized they had been outsmarted by a jackass, they were so outraged and offended that they took back all the corn, every morsel—the hull, the husk, and the stalk. And the sharpest-winged of them snatched the blue velvet hat, which had provided the old mule a po' bit of shade.

The farmer returned at dusk to a bare, dry-grass cornfield and the mule wringing his tail, bluer than blue. The farmer gave the mule a whack on the jaw, shouting, "Come first cockcrow tomorrow, we boils your hooves for backfat and for soap!"

But as soon as the farmer turned his back, the mule tossed the reins from round his neck.

The full moon jangled from a silver chain in the blue-black sky, jazzing. Comets snapped their tails; falling stars blinked and became twice as many, beckoning him to follow, follow.

As he followed high road and branch water, a rosebush brushed his shinbones. He remembered his ma, thoroughbred as they come, cantering up Bourbon Street, under jazz evenings soft as yellow silk.

Under flame-painted sunsets, the sound of saxophones cool as well water, barefoot girls danced in the street with snapping fingers. And Satchmo, wiping with his white kerchief the sweat popping from his brow, blared blues and hues cold on his trumpet.

"Well, I believes my luck's done turned," exclaimed the mule, "as grass is green, sho' nuff done turned.

"I believes . . . I believes I gon' play the trumpet on Bourbon Street, down in New Orleans!"

BRAYYYYYYYYY!

As he spoke, grasshoppers played fiddle on their knees, ring-tailed roarers bebopped hymns with tall tail talk in the middle of a baritone toad's *brrump, brrump, brrump,* and crawdads clicked their claws.

Delighted, the mule pinned back his ears and joined in.

"BRAYYYYYYYYY!" he trumpeted, and shadows jumped six feet, then ten feet.

Owls hooted in harmony, "OOhooooo, OOhoooo."

"Hmmph! Wit' a trumpet like this, I guarantees Satchmo hisself would travel river and round just to hear me play," bragged the mule.

He sojourned down a grassy river bend and across the knotty pine bridge rattling over it, where he chanced upon a curious thing. Among a patch of yam and cheek-tall grass, underneath a sweet gum tree, a bloodhound pawed up dust and dirt. The moon rolled silver under a sleeping cloud, and suddenly the night darkened to pitch. The hound threw back his head.

"*ARRRRRRRRRRRRRRRROOOOOOUUU*," he howled into the deep, dark dark.

And the pecan trees and the palmetto trees and the black persimmon trees echoed "*ARRRRRRRRRRRRRRRROOOOOOUUU*" too as the moon rolled back.

"What's the word, blood?" asked the mule.

"Ain't no thing but a chicken wing," returned the hound, dragging from the hole a sorry-looking bone.

"You got a puss long as a polecat's scent," remarked the mule.

"You'd have one too, if you was in my shoes," retorted the dog. "For years I was man's best friend. I led the hunt for fox and beaver and rabbit and mink. I beat them rattlesnakes a mile. But the years done caught my gray hairs, and my nose ain't what it used to be.

"Tomorrow I is to be hanged on yonder peach tree to make room for young blood a-come to take my place. But me and my bone, we takin' the high road."

ARRRRRRRRRRRRRRRROOOOOOOUUU!

"Better high road than low road," said the mule.

"Better one road than no road," said the dog.

"Better buzzard glide than one step back."

"Better huckle-buck diddy bop walk she-bop."

"What you say," said the mule with a laugh. "A fly don't look by, and a grin saves yo' skin.

"Look-a here, Brother Hound," the mule went on, "why not come wit' me? I's goin' to Bourbon Street to play on the corner, hoe down and git down. You play the bones, scat, croon, and doo-wop doo-wop, so come wit' me."

"Sho' nuff?" asked the hound.

"As grass is green, sho' nuff," replied the mule, and the two new friends highstepped road.

The mule and the hound wandered down river bend, down gully root and wild grapevine swings, down the peapod leaves and pea vine eaves, till they heard a hollerin'.

Atop a stack o' hay, a ragged rooster crowed.

"Upon my soul, Reb'n Chanticleer—" began the mule. But the rooster tilted his head and swiveled his neck and crowed, "COCK-A-DOODLE-DOO!" so long and hard that leaves on graveyard bushes and cypress trees trembled and hid their green, the pray bugs were scandalized, and rusty tree frogs fled the valley.

"You sets my tail on edge," said the mule. "Why all the hullaballoos?"

"And why is you preachin' moon-up 'stead of sun-up?" inquired the hound.

"Don't you be tellin' me my business, boy," snapped the rooster. "Moon ain't worryin' me none.

"Before the years brushed my feathers gray," he continued, "I be the clock the world revolved around. I crowed at sun-up, I crowed when the ice come … I crowed when the sun melt the dust, and when chicks cracked out of shells, and when chinaberry trees danced green sleeves. I read the winds and the rains and the passage o' time, an' I crowed an' I crowed an' I crowed, callin' all them busybody hens to come, and come roost.

"Then everything went to seed."

Here the Reverend stopped to flick a bit of yellow dust off his tail feathers.

"First, bad weather cut us, then the cow went dry, and the corn crops failed, and the foxes and possums robbed the missus blind. How deep can the bottom go?"

"Them what don't look sometime gets took," remarked the hound.

"Mmmmm, mmmm, mmmm," murmured the mule.

"Tomorrow I is to swing by the neck till it snaps, then be popped in a pot wit' onions and dumplings and smothered in gravy for Sunday supper," concluded the rooster. "So I preaches whiles I still can."

"Come wit' us," said the mule. "We is a-travelin' to Bourbon Street to play ragtime and cut the rug. You understand the blues an' you can bass it, you sho' nuff can bass it, so come wit' us."

"Sho' nuff?" asked the rooster.

"As grass is green, sho' nuff," said the mule and the hound. And the three highstepped road toward Bourbon Street.

By and by the mule, the dog, and the rooster paused by the edge of the bayou to take a sip of water, and there they spied a ginger cat.

She batted her paws at a dusty rat who slunk by laughing as she missed his tail.

"See here, sister," said the mule.

"Git back, jack!" hissed the cat, for she had caught the scent of a field mouse scurrying along the magnolia trees by the water's edge. Closer and closer she crept, until all at once she sprang—*splash!* But all she snatched was its shadow dancing across the water, and the bayou rained mud and swamp water, splattering the cat, the dog, the rooster, and the mule.

"MEEEOWWWW!" the ginger cat yowled, and shook herself dry.

"Rain? In the middle of July?" asked the hound.

"Phhhfffft, laugh!" snorted the cat. "You wouldn't if you wore my boots!

"I spent my days on the mistress's lap, wit' my own silk pillow, warm cream, and all the butterfish I could eat from my very own silver bowl.

"But times is hard, and the mistress lost all the money she had. Now my claws aren't as sharp as they used to be before the years spun my whiskers gray. These days when I leap, I don't always land on my feet. Sometimes it's nose-first." She shook her head. "Come cockcrow tomorrow, Mistress wants to drown me in the river, because I can no longer earn my keep."

MEEEOWWWW!

"Why not come wit' us?" invited
the mule. "We is goin' to Bourbon Street to bebop and
jazz. You can carry a tune and you have a bit of the torch in your
song, so come wit' us, and we'll mardi gras and hi-de-ho."

"Sho' nuff?" asked the cat.

"As grass is green, sho' nuff," answered the rest.

And so they traveled on through the Spanish moss, through
a swarm of green dragonflies, through scissoring foolish fireflies
flicking light in every tree hollow, and past sugar cane so high
it brushed the edge of the hot indigo sky crackling jade, copper,
indigo.

Presently they came to a crossroads: to the left a zigzag trail, to the right the wind-washed boards of a crawfisher's shack. The four friends couldn't decide which way to go.

"Let's try here," suggested the mule. "Someone's bound to know."

The others liked the idea for, as the cat said, better to ask once than to get lost twice, having gone several half miles and the night not getting any shorter.

The mule, being the tallest, stepped up to investigate. He pressed his nose against the glass and peered through the gap in the curtains.

"Well, what does ya sees?" asked the hound.

"What does I sees?" echoed the mule. "I sees a table spread wit' gumbo ya-ya, couché-couché, cornpone, crowder peas wit' snaps, fatback grease, redeye gravy, and pralines and ice cream, wit' a jug of wild persimmon brew.

"*And* four roughnecks eatin' wit' jackknives and thumbs.

"*And* one on a footstool scratchin' on a fiddle wit' a stick.

"*And* one in the corner countin' pearls in a gunnysack:

　　Un, deux, trois,

　　un, deux, trois,

thicker than thieves."

"Ain't it gettin' on *our* suppertime?" asked the hound.

"Quarter past nine, and goin' on a biscuit," answered the mule. "I do believe it's time."

"And since," added the rooster.

"Since *and* since," sniffed the cat.

"Back where I come from," mused the mule, "you gots to sing for your supper."

"Back where I come from, you gots to howl," declared the hound.

"You gots to crow," retorted the rooster.

"You gots to yowl," snapped the cat.

"Surprise 'em with a ditty or two, or three, an' they'll invite us to supper," returned the mule. "You'll see."

ARRRRRRRRR

So the hound clambered on the mule's back, the cat perched on top of the dog, and the rooster swayed on the cat's shoulder. The mule pawed the soil, *patoom*, *patoom*, and swished his tail.

And then the mule trumpeted, "BRRAAYYYY!" BeBOP BOP.

The hound howled, "ARRRRRRRRRRRRROOOOOUUU!" BeBOP BOP.

The rooster crowed, "COCK-A-DOODLE-DOO!" BeBOP BOP.

The cat yowled so high, the sound broke the windowpanes and flipped the moon over—heads, tails—"MEEEOOWWWW!" BeBOP BOP.

29

The four friends jumped through the window, *Boom! Crash! Buffalo!* BeBOP BOP.

"*Whoo-wee!* That sounded fine!" exclaimed the mule.

"Right fine," echoed the hound.

"Ain't heard nothin' as fine," said the rooster.

"Not in a coon's age," agreed the cat.

They looked round for their invitation to supper, but to their surprise, the thieves had dropped their pearls, peas, and pone and fled to the bayou.

"Hmmmph! Well, it's an ill wind blows nobody good," huffed the cat as she took a huge helping of peas. The other three nodded as they licked up the gumbo ya-ya, and they all ate till they couldn't anymore.

And when they had finished feasting, they found places to pillow their heads. The mule nestled on a bed of leaves in the yard, the hound snuggled behind the back door, the cat curled up beside the warm ashes of the woodstove in the kitchen, and the rooster roosted on the roof, as roosters do.

Gold-tipped butterflies fluttered over pea-colored cattails growing deep, palmettos rattled and clacked, and the moon made diamonds of leaves and light.

Whuush, whuush, a warm wind whistled in trees tall as twilight.

Whuush, whuush, and the four friends slept under the lullaby of night, at peace and very nearly content.

Meanwhile, the thieves sat scowling aboard their riverboat on the curve of the bayou. The night was so peaceful, they could hear dewdrops whistle on the backs of boll weevils.

"It wasn't a loup-garou," the bravest one argued, "or a ghost, but only the swift elbow of the wind knockin' about."

They sat undecided till the bravest one said, "I'm tired o' starin' at our boots! I say we goes back for our pearls."

So they sneaked back through shadows, and the others hid behind a chinaberry tree while the bravest crept up to the house.

He stepped into the kitchen to strike a light and, thinking the fiery eyes of the cat to be live coals, held a stick of sulfur to them to light his match. But the cat leaped into his face, scratching and spitting.

The thief cried out in a panic and tried to escape by the back door but stumbled over the hound, who snarled and gave him a ferocious bite on both ankles.

COCK-A-DOODLE-DOO!

"Ouch!" he hollered. He ran out the front door and tripped over the mule, who gave him a sound kick on the seat of his pants and sent him clawing and flailing into the night sky.

Now, the rooster, who had been wakened by the racket, thought it must be morning. Feeling frisky and quite bodacious, he jumped up and flapped and crowed, "COCK-A-DOODLE-DOO!"

As quickly as he could, the thief limped to the chinaberry tree, where his companions were waiting anxiously.

"The pearls?" they cried. "Where are our pearls?"

"Mon Dieu!" he rasped. "In that house there's a witch, a conjure witch. The obeah nearly blinded me as she raked her long red nails down my cheek. I felt her hot breath as she spat incantations of hoodoo and flung the gris-gris into my face.

"By the back door stands the loup-garou, who stabbed me in both ankles wit' his hunting knife, and in the yard a bogeyman knocked me sideways wit' his battlin' stick.

"And on the rooftop sits the judge, who cries: 'Lock them up two by two! Lock them up two by two!'

"I ran with the wind at my back, and I'd advise y'all to do the same."

And so they all disappeared, chased by the wind.

As for the four musicians, they found that time had never passed as passable as it did in that li'l crawfish shack, and so they decided not to venture to Bourbon Street after all, but to spend the rest of their days there on the bayou among the lilies, weevils, and fireflies, eatin' grits and gravy.

Mos' likely they be there still, playin' the bones and howlin' down the moon to dance on a song and a dare.

Sho' nuff?

As grass is green, sho' nuff, y'all.

GLOSSARY

backfat: fat from the upper part of an animal

bayou: a stream-fed swamp or marsh

Bourbon Street: famous street in New Orleans where musicians perform

buzzard glide, huckle-buck: jazz dances

conjure witch: a woman who practices sorcery

cornpone: a fried or baked cornbread cake

couché-couché: Cajun fried spoonbread or cornmeal mush

crawdad: crayfish

crowder peas: a variety of peas eaten in the South

gris-gris: magic charm

gumbo ya-ya: hot and spicy Louisiana seafood stew

hoodoo: powerful spells

loup-garou: werewolf

Mardi gras: a holiday celebrated in New Orleans with costumes, dancing, and parades

obeah: a wise witch woman

play the bones: make music by clicking dry bones together

polecat: skunk

pralines: candy made of nuts and sugar

redeye gravy: ham gravy

ring-tailed roarer: rowdy and boastful backwoodsman who believed himself to be part animal

Satchmo: nickname of Louis Armstrong, famous African American jazz musician, legendary for his New Orleans-style trumpet playing

scat: improvised jazz singing using syllables and sounds

un, deux, trois: French for "one, two, three"

Clarion Books • a Houghton Mifflin Company imprint • 215 Park Avenue South, New York, NY 10003

Text copyright © 2002 by Kathy Price • Illustrations copyright © 2002 by Andrew Glass

The illustrations were executed in oil crayon and turpenoid. • The text was set in 20-point Pike.

Printed in Singapore.

Library of Congress Cataloging-in-Publication Data

Price, Kathy (Kathy Z.)

The Bourbon Street musicians / by Kathy Price ; illustrated by Andrew Glass.

p. cm.

Summary: A Cajun retelling of the classic tale of four animals, past their prime, who set out together to become musicians.

ISBN 0-618-04076-5

[1. Fairy tales. 2. Folklore—Germany.] I. Glass, Andrew, ill. II. Bremen town musicians. III. Title.

PZ8.P92 Bo 2002 • [398.2]—dc21 • 2001028892

TWP 10 9 8 7 6 5 4 3 2 1